W·H·I·T·E·F·O·O·T

Whitefoot

A *Story* FROM THE *Center* OF THE *World*

Wendell Berry

Illustrations by Davis Te Selle

COUNTERPOINT

BERKELEY

This book is a work of fiction.
Nothing is in it that has not been imagined.

The story "Whitefoot" was first published in *Orion Magazine*.

Berry, Wendell, 1934–
Whitefoot : a story from the center of the world / Wendell Berry ;
illustrations by Davis Te Selle.
p. cm.
Summary: A white-footed mouse is swept away in a flood and must carefully watch and wait
until it is safe to make a home in its new surroundings.
Hardcover ISBN: 978-1-58243-432-2
Paperback ISBN: 978-1-58243-640-1
1. Peromyscus leucopus—Juvenile fiction. [1. White-footed mouse—
Fiction. 2. Mice—Fiction.] I. Te Selle, David, ill. II. Title.
PZ10.3.B4553wh 2009
[Fic]—dc22   2008035706

Book design by David Bullen
Printed in Canada

COUNTERPOINT
1919 Fifth Street
Berkeley, CA 94710
www.counterpointpress.com

Distributed by Publishers Group West

10 9 8 7 6 5 4 3 2 1

Whitefoot

A *Story* FROM THE *Center*
OF THE *World*

Her name was *Peromyscus leucopus,* but she did not know it. I think it had been a long time since the mice around Port William spoke English, let alone Latin. Her language was a dialect of Mouse, a tongue for which we humans have never developed a vocabulary or a grammar. Because I don't know her name in Mouse, I will call her Whitefoot.

The name fits because her four small feet and all the underside of her were a pure, clean white. Her coat, above, was a reddish brindly tan. She had a graceful tail, a set of long elegant whiskers, perfect ever-listening ears, a fastidious nose, and black profound eyes shining with sight. She took a small feminine pleasure in being beautiful.

She was born in the fall, and now the winter was ending. In the spring, if she escaped her many enemies, she would have her first litter of maybe six baby mice. In comparison to a white oak, or even a human, she would not live long, perhaps not a year, almost certainly not two, but the little life she had she loved dearly and so far she had taken excellent care of it. She had fed herself well on nuts and seeds and insects. She had kept herself clean and neat. She had been cautious and clever in keeping herself out of the sight of larger creatures. She was highly skilled in being a mouse.

She lived at the briary edge of a wooded hollow on what was known as the old Keith place in the bottomland not far from Port William—but she did not know that either. She did not know that only a few hundred yards away the river ran between its high, wooded banks. Her native country was about an acre of ground overhung by about an acre of sky crisscrossed by grassblades, weedstems, the stems and twigs of low bushes, and the limbs of trees.

Her acre of ground was as crisscrossed by her comings and goings as her acre of sky by all the blades and stems and branches overhead. In her busy life, always looking for things to eat, she had been everywhere in her small homeland. But if you had gone there, though she might easily have seen you, you would almost certainly not have seen her, for she went quickly, quietly, mostly at night, and in paths and ways that went deep in amongst the other lives of that place. Sometimes in her search for food she might climb a dozen or so feet into a tree

or bush, but everywhere she meant to be unseen by any creature larger than herself.

To imagine the life and adventures of Whitefoot, you must compress your mind to her size. Think of going about with your eyes only an inch or two from the ground, among grass stems thicker than your thumb, weed stems thicker than your wrist, maple and oak leaves that you can slip under and hide, trees that touch the sky.

She lived at the center of the world. This is one of the things every mouse knows. Wherever she was, she was at the center of the world. That one lives at the center of the world is the world's profoundest thought. So firmly was this thought set in Whitefoot's mind that she did not need to think it. Like humans, she lived in the little world of what she knew, for there was no other world for her to live in. But she lived at the center of her world always, and of this she had no doubt.

Wherever she was, she was at the center of the world

She had spent the winter with several of her relatives in a cavity among the roots of a dead tree. They huddled together for warmth when it was cold. They slept long sleeps. They went about in small paths and tunnels under the grass and fallen leaves, and under the snow, to secret hollows sheltered from the wet where they had stored their autumn harvest of small acorns and other seeds.

But then as the days grew longer and March came, Whitefoot began to hear in her mind a voice speaking in Mouse. This was the same voice that would sometimes say to her, "Seeds! Seeds!" and sometimes, "Look out!" But now, as spring approached, it said, "Nest! Nest!" And so she left the community burrow where she had wintered and set out on her own.

She was looking for a dry hollow place to make a

home for herself and eventually for her children. The hollow she finally chose was not one you would have expected from knowing the history and the habits of her race. It was the inside of a large round glass jar left on her acre when the river had flooded several years before. The lid of the jar was screwed on tightly, but somehow a hole had been knocked in the glass below the jar's shoulder. It was a hole shaped like an eye, just big enough for a mouse to enter. As the jar lay among

the grasses and dead leaves on the floor of the thicket, the hole was toward the downward side, so that the rain did not run into it. The jar was the right size for a nest. It was not what she was used to, but as mice live entirely by opportunity, Whitefoot took it. She went in and moved around, sniffing and looking, and came out, and went in again, and came out. It would do.

The voice that had been saying, "Nest! Nest!" now began to say, "Hurry! Hurry!" She went darting about in her hidden pathways, and out, more dangerously, onto the surfaces of the woods floor. She gathered dry grass, pieces of dead leaves, strands of bark, a few soft feathers from a blue jay that a hawk had eaten, some bright tufts of moss. She made many trips to her jar, carrying these valuable things in her mouth, and put them inside. She went in darts and starts, often stopping to look and sniff and listen, for the voice in her mind that was saying

She had to hurry, but also she had to listen

"Nest!" and "Hurry!" also frequently would say "Look out!" The leaves had not yet unfolded from their buds. The grass had not begun to grow. She did her work often in full view of the sky—and also, it might have been, within the vision of an owl or a fox. She had to hurry, but she also had to listen. She had to watch.

When she had filled her jar with all the things she had gathered, she burrowed in and made a little hollow, a place for herself just the size of herself, in the center of it. With her forefeet, which were as cunning as hands, she combed her building materials into place. She shredded them and made them fine with her teeth. She nudged and compacted them with her nose and her feet. She molded the cup of the nest exactly to fit by pressing against it with her body. She made it snug. She did her work according to an ancient, honorable principle: Enough is enough. She worked and lived without extravagance and without waste. Her nest was a neat small cup the size of herself asleep. When she went into it for her daytime sleep, she slept drawn into a ball, her eyes shut, her tail curved around so that its outer end lay under her nose. Her sleep was an act of faith and a giving of thanks.

While the nest was still new, rain began to fall. The sunlight disappeared, the sky was darkened by low clouds, and it rained and rained. When the rain stopped, the trees dripped big drops onto the dead leaves, and then it rained again, sometimes gently, sometimes hard. Whitefoot went about in the wet darkness of the nights, finding food, and when the gray daylight came she returned to her home in the old jar, curled up in the soft cup of her nest, and went to sleep.

One day as she slept, a change began to happen, and it

went on happening. Into the sound of raindrops falling onto the tree branches overhead and the sodden layer of dead leaves on the ground came the new sound of rain falling onto water. That sound grew wider and nearer as Whitefoot slept. An uneasy dream as large as the world she knew caused her to quiver in her sleep.

In the middle of the afternoon she woke, for the bottom end of her jar had lifted slightly from its resting place. The voice in her mind had called into her sleep, "Look out!" And then it had said, "Hurry!"

She went to the broken opening in the jar and looked out. The day was silvery with mist, the tree trunks black against it, fading into it. The rain was falling through the mist. Beyond, disappearing into the mist, lay a broad sheet of water gleaming with pale daylight, littered with floating things. The water began to seep and then to flow into Whitefoot's jar. She leapt out, and she sank. The voice in her mind said, "Up!" and she began to swim. She saw that beyond her jar the ground still rose above the water, and she swam toward the higher ground.

She swam and then waded until she was out of the water and the sound of the rain had changed around her. But she was not safe. She was on an island only a few feet across, and the island was getting smaller. As she huddled, wet and bewildered on the soggy leaves, the

water kept rising. She was forced at last to climb onto a small log. She did not like to do that, for it made her easy to be seen by whatever might be looking, but there was no choice. She crouched on the log, making herself as small as she could, and kept still. From creatures that walked she had for the time being nothing to fear. They were as much occupied with saving themselves as she was. The weasels, minks, cats, skunks, raccoons, and foxes, like Whitefoot herself, would be trying to keep above the rising water. But she also had enemies who flew: in daylight the hawks, at night the owls. As she huddled on her log, she shivered because she was wet and cold, and also because she was afraid. She watched and waited, for that was all she could do. After a while, her log began to float.

She had never floated before, but when the water lifted the log from the ground she knew at once that she

was floating. As it came free of the ground, the log rolled somewhat into its new balance on the water, and she had to clamber onto the top of it again to keep from falling off. The sound of rain falling on water was all around her now. And through the treetops overhead the wind moved and made an airy sound.

As the wind blew, the log carried Whitefoot slowly out of her home acre. Bobbing on the small waves the wind made, now and again snagging on weed stems or low bushes and then turning past them, the log carried her toward the river.

She did not move. The safest thing she could do was to keep as still "as a knot on a log" and she did. Only the log moved. It moved with the motions of the water and the wind.

A red-bellied woodpecker watched from his hole in

a dead locust tree as Whitefoot floated by. Over the woodpecker's hole a bracket fungus shelved out like a porch roof.

For a little while the log floated free of trees. The wind blew it across part of a cornfield. A flock of wild turkeys were feeding in the field, walking slowly away from the rising water. And though this was surely the unhappiest day of Whitefoot's life, a pair of wood ducks was dabbling cheerfully over the submerged corn rows.

Nearer the river, a great blue heron was standing as still as a post. And then, stabbing into the water with its long beak, it caught a fish and swallowed it.

Later, as the water deepened beneath Whitefoot's log, a muskrat swam by at the point of the V it made along the surface. It dived, and for a second only its tail was in sight, curved like a question mark, and then the tail too disappeared.

Whitefoot, who could not fly and did not wish to swim, floated among trees again, as the wind pushed her log out toward the river. Except for shivering, she did not move. She only watched as the log floated and nudged against obstacles and paused and turned and floated on. If you had seen her, you might have thought she was being patient. She was capable of patience, I think, but now she was simply doing nothing, which was all there was to do.

Her log did not touch land again or any larger log. It did not bump against anything she might have climbed onto. It went slowly along, moving away from the wind, and the motions it made gave Whitefoot the floating feeling that was new to her. This feeling kept her alert. She was not going to get used to it.

A change of light came over her, for the wind had shoved her log finally out into the open river. Such a length of sky as Whitefoot had never seen opened suddenly above her between the two long lines of trees standing in deep water on what had been the river's banks. Now the water beneath her log was swift and troubled, not only by the wind, but by the hundred different shifts and whirls of the current. The light came down on the water, and the water flung it upward again, filling the air with quick gleams and reflections.

Now all around her, in addition to the sounds of the

rain falling on the water and the wind in the branches was the louder sound of the swift currents slurring past the trunks of the trees.

In the river, the log was less pushed by the wind than carried along by the moving water. It is easy to think of a flowing river as having one current, but actually the current is made of many currents flowing at different speeds and in different directions, crisscrossing, whirling, braiding together.

At first, Whitefoot's log drifted by itself, the currents turning it as they carried it on. But when the motions of water and wind had moved it out into the channel, the main force of the flow, it began to be accompanied by other floating things, by the rubble of woods and fields and by human rubbish: twigs and leaves, bits of dead grass, cornstalks, sticks, scraps of lumber, cans and bottles, logs, tree limbs, pieces of plastic foam, barrels, old tires, a basketball, whole trees. These things whirled along separately or in large mats of drift that were like floating rugs.

These mats gathered sometimes until they were many feet across, until they were rafts, and then the currents tore or whirled them apart, and then they were regathered into new shapes. But some were more tightly bound together by logs or by the trunks and limbs of large trees. Finally it happened that Whitefoot's log was caught up into one of these, a raft of drift held together by the roots and sprawling branches of an old water maple that had been released by a collapsing bank upstream. Though its surface lifted and fell with the motions of the water, and though it was constantly fraying at the edges, because of the big tree this raft of drift was more sturdy than most. It was like a floating island. Several golden-eyed blackbirds were confidently walking on it, feeding and looking around.

I don't believe Whitefoot would have thought of imitating the birds, whose long, spreading toes held them up on that floating chaff as securely as if it were solid ground, and who anyhow could fly to safety if they needed to. I think Whitefoot merely knew that her own small feet needed something more solid. She did not move, though if she could have done so she would have climbed upward, away from the terrible nearness of the water.

When the rain quit, the surface of the river became glossy, littered with scraps and splinters of reflected light. When the rain dashed down again, the folds and ripples of the surface roughened like goose flesh.

All the rest of that day, while the risen water carried her maybe fifteen miles, Whitefoot did not move. She

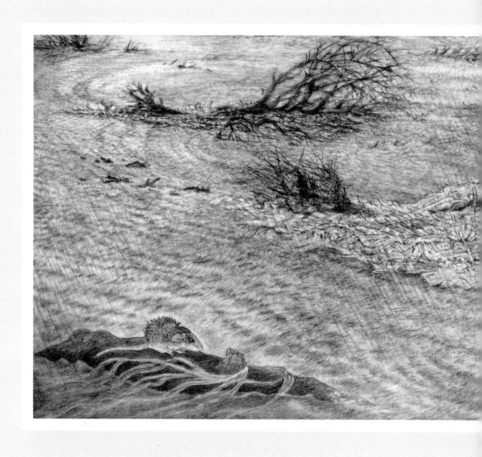

It was like a floating island

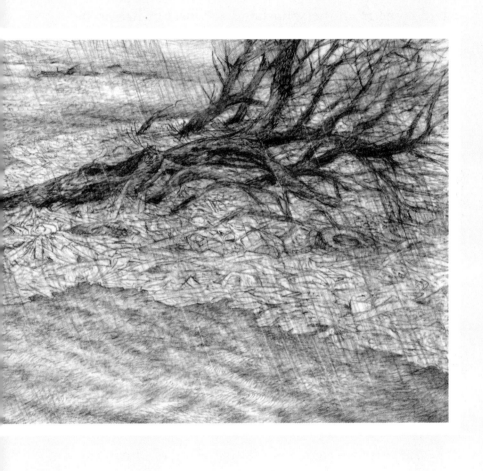

had come from the solid familiar world of her home acre into this strange, never-resting world of water and air and light, where everything was changing all the time. She was wet and cold and bewildered and frightened, and she knew that all the safety she had was in keeping still.

For a while several coots fed eagerly, tipping and diving, among the mats of drift. And where the river flowed past a submerged creek mouth, a family of otters was traveling upstream through the quieter water, looping through the surface as they went. Whitefoot's eyes lingered on nothing. As the river carried and turned her, she saw what she saw. In the late afternoon the light changed around her again as she passed out of the mouth of the first river and entered a much wider one. As the currents carried her flimsy island out into midchannel of the larger river, Whitefoot felt she was in a world entirely watery and flowing. The trees of the shorelines and bottomlands were far on either side and were veiled by mist and the falling rain. Whitefoot's eyes, used to the enclosed world of the woods where she had always lived, could hardly see so far. She could hardly know that way off, beyond the edges of the water, the land still rose up firm. All she knew now was the moving water, the shifting light on the water, the rain, and the wind. The wind was driving large waves upstream against the flowing of the river. The mat of drift rose and fell as the waves rolled under it.

The voice in Whitefoot's mind cried, "Look out! Look out!" But there was nothing to do, no place to go, no dry hole to creep into and be safe and get dry and grow warm and go to sleep. She clung, hunched down and shivering, to the little log as it tilted over the waves, seeing only the great light and the turning, swaying drift.

As evening came, the wind ceased and the water slowly became smoother. A little comfort came to Whitefoot, though she was still wet and cold and frightened. She was hungry too. And now as the day darkened and the night rose into the eastward mist, she was coming to her waking time. It was time to be up and about.

If you had been there, and were able to see in the dark,

you would have seen Whitefoot change as night fell on the river. She changed from a small, huddled animal who might as well have been asleep to an animal altogether awake. Her eyes, that had been seeing only what the daylight and the moving river showed her, now had purpose in them and they were looking. Her ears were listening into the slur and spatter around her. Her nose was intelligently sniffing. Even her whiskers had grown alert. Though she had not yet moved, she was clearly an animal ready to move. The voice in her mind was saying, "Seeds! Seeds! Look around!"

Even if you could see in the dark, you would have had to look fast to see her move. You would have seen her in the middle of her log, and then you would have seen her at one of the ends of it. And then you would have seen her in several stops on her way to the other end. She was moving in darts and starts as always. It would have seemed to you as if she simply disappeared in one place and reappeared in another. She had begun her nightly hunt for food, and she needed to escape from her log where she had found not a thing to eat. At the end of the log she first went to there was nothing that would support even her little weight, just a thin, flimsy, soggy carpet of floating grass and leaves and small twigs. When she got to the other end a wave caused her log to bump against something that her senses told her was solid. It was an old tire, and she leaped onto it.

With the same small darts and starts as before, she made her way around the tire and then perhaps two-thirds of the way around again. She leaped onto a broken oar, and from there to a one-armed plastic doll, and from there to another log. She explored the length of this new log and found that it reached into what had once been the top of the old water maple itself. Whitefoot leaped

again and grappled her way up among the branches. As she climbed about, she propped and balanced herself with her tail.

The flower buds of the old tree were fattening, ready to break into bloom. Whitefoot paused here and there to nibble these as she made her way from thin branches to branches that became stouter as she got nearer to the main trunk. Once she had reached a sturdy branch and was traveling along it toward the trunk, she understood that she was safer than she had been before. The great tree moved with the current, but the big waves did not affect it much, the small ones not at all.

When Whitefoot got to the trunk of the tree, which was more than half submerged in the water, she worked her way carefully along it, exploring it as a new territory, but she was also searching for food. She inquired into the creases and under the flakes of the bark. The tree trunk bore a wound where a large branch had broken off. There, where the wood had begun to rot, she found two small beetles, and she ate them. In another place she found the larva of a moth, and she ate that. She worked her way along the trunk of the tree all the way to the upward sprangle of the roots, and then she hunted among the roots. She found a few things to eat, but nowhere did she find enough to make a meal.

It was a dark night. To us, it would have seemed as black as a bucket of tar, but for Whitefoot, as she went about in her search, smell and touch worked as well as sight. She did not need to see.

For a long time she heard only the sounds of the flowing river and of the rain falling on the water. And then she heard in the distance downstream a low hum that grew louder, and she saw a glow that grew brighter. As

the sound became a heavy drumming as wide as the water and the darkness, the glow gathered into a brilliant point of light that cast a bright beam onto the river. The noise grew closer and louder. The light shone on Whitefoot's log and she again became still, a frightened small bump.

The towboat with its immense bulk of loaded barges went by with a crashing sound, and then Whitefoot's floating island was in the dark again, and the boat's wake was heaving even the big water maple up and down. Whitefoot kept still until the water quieted and the sound of the boat's engines was again only a hum and her fear had passed. And then she resumed her foraging.

She stayed hungry and she continued to hunt. She did not hunt systematically, as you and I might have done, going over the great tree trunk inch by inch. If she had done that, she would have been more thorough, but also she would have been easier to catch. The voice in her mind was always warning her to look, to be alert. As always before, she moved in quick starts and darts, pausing here and there to sniff for something edible, but never pausing for long.

In that way, appearing to hurry, but really taking her time, she made her way from the roots of the tree back

again toward the branches. The top of the tree, like the trunk, was half submerged. But several large limbs reached high up into the air, branching out and out finally into thin twigs with flower and leaf buds at their ends. Whitefoot ate some more of the buds. But by the time the dawn light began to whiten the eastern sky, she had found two things that were better than all the rest.

She found, first, a deep knothole sheltered from the rain and the wind. And then she found a stash of chinquapin acorns, wild cherry seeds, and corn grains, stored by a flying squirrel in an old woodpecker hole. She made a full meal at last, and then as the night was ending she crept into the very bottom of the knothole. She made a bed there on the soft, dry powder of rotted wood. Curled snugly, with the end of her tail under her nose, she fell into a day-long sleep.

Morning brightened the mist over the river

As morning brightened the mist over the river, a pair of wild geese sailed down together, like two arrows shot, and sliced the surface of the water as they touched it and settled, and then they floated quietly, dignified and alert. Whitefoot did not see them. When other tow-boats passed, rocking the old tree where she slept, she did not awaken. She did not see the sun brighten the mist to a blinding whiteness and finally shine through it, glittering and glaring on the water. She did not see the pair of green-winged teal who rode for a while on the trunk of her tree, the drake's green eye patch gleaming in the sunlight. She did not see the pied-billed grebe fishing in an eddy, as steadfast in the current as if anchored. She did not see the quick curving of its neck as it seemed to leap through the surface of the river. She did not see it reappear with a caught fish that it gaped and lunged upward to swallow. She did not know when the current carried her past a city with bridges.

She slept too through another change in her story. In the afternoon, as the old maple with Whitefoot asleep inside it was carried down a long southward passage, the wind began to blow hard from the east. The tree's limbs and even its buds caught the wind. Now the island of drift was like a boat with a sail. The wind moved it slowly westward out of the current, and finally out of the river and into the still backwater over the bottomland.

When Whitefoot woke up at nightfall, she no longer heard the sounds of the flowing river, but only the sound of the wind moving in the bare branches of trees. The raft of drift, now much smaller and still raveling apart, had been blown against the thickety edge of a grove of trees and the old maple had lodged there. Whitefoot's travels had ended; her tree was going no farther. But this

Whitefoot's travels had ended

story had not ended yet, for the tree and the drift that still clung to it was no less an island than it had been before. Water was all around it. Many acres of water, gleaming in the light of the growing moon, rippled as the air stirred over it.

That night, as before, she searched for food among the roots and along the trunk and among the branches of the floating tree. She fed. She was taking, hour by hour, the opportunity to live. At dawn she returned to the knothole and went to sleep.

The next night and the night after that were much the same. But toward the end of the fourth night a terrible shadow fell between Whitefoot and the moon. The voice in her mind cried, "Look out!" Perhaps she moved in time, but even so one of the heel talons of the owl struck her and tumbled her off the tree trunk into the water. She had to swim, struggling in the floating carpet of sticks and leaves, for several minutes before she could clamber back onto her tree. The day dawned and she slept again.

That day the flood began to subside. The old tree shifted and jolted, breaking the limbs beneath it as it settled toward the ground. But more nights had to pass before the water drew away beneath the tree. Whitefoot's hunting and exploring became more anxious, for

she was running out of food. Now when she went to sleep at the night's end she was hungry. It rained, and it cleared again, and the water continued to draw back from the land.

When the tree finally came to rest on the ground, Whitefoot knew it. She was asleep, but the floating feeling left her and she woke up. She left her knothole, and though it was not yet completely dark, she began to look around. The trunk of the old maple was some distance from the ground, held up by its roots and branches as if on legs, and water was still puddled under it. Whitefoot finally found a long branch that led out beyond the edge of the water, and she followed it down onto the wet world.

It would be days yet before the place would be dry and familiar to her, but already she was confident. She left at first a line of little tracks across the mud, and then she went into a dank space beneath the bent and muddied grasses of the woods edge. And then she came out again and looked around and disappeared again. The voice in her mind was speaking to her of her needs. She needed food. She needed a nesting place. She needed dry ground.

At the center of the world, on the silted and soiled floor of the woods, among the shadows of the moony night, she went about her still-unfinished task of staying alive.